C L A

DRACULA

RETOLD BY
MICK GOWAR

ILLUSTRATED BY
WILDMAN

First published in 2011 by
Franklin Watts
338 Euston Road
London NW1 3BH

Franklin Watts Australia
Level 17/207 Kent Street
Sydney NSW 2000

A CIP catalogue record for this book
is available from the British Library.

ISBN 978 1 4451 0460 7

Dewey Classification: 823.9'14

1 3 5 7 9 10 8 6 4 2

Picture acknowledgements: Cover: Ekaterina Fribus/Shutterstock: b.
Ew Chee Guan/Shutterstock: t. M T Kang/Shutterstock: cr.
Margaret M Stewart/Shutterstock: c. p.46: Mary Evans Picture Library/Alamy

Printed in Great Britain

Franklin Watts is a division of Hachette Children's Books,
an Hachette UK company.
www.hachette.co.uk

Contents

A LETTER

To my dearest daughter Lucy,

I am writing you this long letter to tell you a little about our family history. I want to tell you about the time when your mother and I were married. But mostly, I want to tell you about why we named you Lucy.

Lucy was the name of your mother's dearest friend. She died in a sad and terrifying way. What happened to Lucy was so frightening that I do not want you to read this letter until you reach your 18th birthday.

What I have to tell you may sound far-fetched, even ridiculous. But believe me, my dearest Lucy, every word is true.

From your loving father,
Jonathan.

CHAPTER ONE
WELCOME TO CASTLE DRACULA

The story begins in 1897. Your mother and I
were engaged to be married. I was a young
lawyer, working in London. I'd just been
given my first proper job: to go all the way to
the remote region of Transylvania in the
country of Romania. I was to visit a very
important client who wished to buy a big
house near London. This client was a very
rich man: Count Dracula. His name sends
shivers down my spine even now.

You can imagine my excitement! It was the
first time I'd been out of England, the first
time I'd travelled by boat, the first time I
could speak the French and German I'd
learnt at school.

I enjoyed every minute of my trip until
I reached the village of Bistritz in Romania.
There my sleep was plagued with terrible
nightmares.

I dreamed of wolves howling and huge bats whose leathery wings clattered and battered at my window.

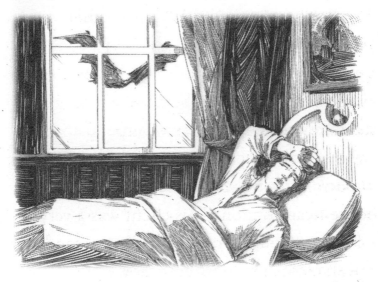

I was glad to get up in the morning. When I told the innkeeper and his wife that I was going to Castle Dracula, they muttered something in Romanian that I didn't understand. The wife then took a silver crucifix from her neck. In her few words of German she begged me to wear it. I tried to refuse, but she insisted and placed the crucifix around my neck.

That afternoon I made my way to the place high in the mountains where the Count was sending his coach to meet me. The journey took longer than I had expected, and I reached the pass as night fell.

It was completely dark by the time the Count's coach appeared. It came hurtling along the road at tremendous speed, drawn by four huge black horses. The silent driver was tall and his eyes glowed red, like burning coals.

I climbed aboard the coach. Away we sped, but from the surrounding forest I heard wolves howling, just like in my dream.

Eventually we reached Castle Dracula. Even in the darkness I could see that it was huge. Pointed towers stretched up so high they seemed to vanish into the black sky. Above the huge oak door was a shield, carved into the stone. There were four crowns on the shield, and above the crowns was a bat with its wings spread wide.

I knocked on the door. After a long wait, it was opened by a tall, pale man.

"Welcome to my home," he said. "I am Dracula." He smiled.

I couldn't help noticing how sharp and pointed his teeth looked. And how, in the light of the candle he was carrying, his eyes glowed red.

The Count led me to a large room where my supper was waiting. He watched me eating, but didn't eat anything himself. He was a friendly host, but I was very tired so I was relieved when it was time to go to bed.

The next morning, when I was in my room shaving, Count Dracula appeared. He stood behind me, but when I looked in my shaving mirror, I appeared to be the only person in the room. I was so shocked that I accidentally cut my chin with my razor.

Then something even more disturbing happened. The Count caught sight of the blood trickling down my chin. His eyes suddenly blazed and he grabbed at my throat. But he exposed the crucifix that hung around my neck and, for some reason, that made him draw back.

"You should take more care," said the Count. He then picked up my mirror and smashed it on the ground. "I don't allow mirrors here," he said.

He turned and left the room.

Much shaken, I went downstairs and ate breakfast alone. There was no sign of the Count, so I decided to explore the castle. I walked down every gloomy corridor. I tried door after door, but every one was locked.

Then I found a door that wasn't locked. Opening it, I found myself in a junk room. The air was musty and stuffy. I suddenly felt very tired and sat down on an old couch. I felt myself drift into a dream, half-awake half-asleep. I seemed to dream that three women appeared.

"Let us drink his blood now!" whispered one of the women. Another bent over me. I could feel her sharp teeth on my neck. Vampires! I was terrified, but I did not seem to be able to move.

"Stop!" It was Count Dracula's voice. "Not yet," he said.

Then darkness surrounded me and I slept.

When I awoke, I was in my own bedroom. I jumped out of bed, determined to find the Count and find out what was going on. But the door was locked. I was a prisoner!

From outside, I could hear the sound of hammering, then of something heavy being dragged across the stones. I went to the window. In the courtyard below men were loading big boxes onto a cart. One box was still open. All it contained was earth.

"Help me!" I shouted out to the men.

Dracula appeared in the courtyard. "I'm afraid you are not allowed to leave," he called up to me.

I waited until the last box had been loaded and the cart had been driven out of the courtyard. I climbed out of the window and down the castle wall, holding tightly onto the thick ivy that grew up it.

I ran to the castle gates. They were locked! But a door next to the gates was open. I went into a small, dark room. In the middle of the room was a box with Dracula's family shield on the side, the same shield as the one over the door. The box was half-filled with earth, and lying in the box was Dracula. He seemed to be sleeping, but his eyes were open and his mouth was half-open in a smile. On his lips was fresh blood.

Chapter Two
The Ship of Death

While I was a prisoner in Castle Dracula, your mother, Mina, was on holiday with her best friend, Lucy. Lucy's mother had rented a holiday home in a town called Whitby on the Yorkshire coast. It was far away from the smoke and the stink of London, and the air there was fresh and clean.

Mina and Lucy loved to sit on a little bench at the top of the cliff and watch the ships sail in and out of Whitby harbour. They sometimes walked among the gloomy ruins of an old abbey which was near their holiday home.

Lucy and Mina had only been in their holiday home for a few days when the mysterious ghost ship sailed into Whitby harbour. The ship had sailed from the north through a violent storm. But when the ship arrived in the harbour, none of the sailors on board were alive. The captain had tied himself to the wheel. He must have died as the ship drifted into the port. The only living thing on board was a huge black dog, which jumped from the boat onto the quay and then ran away.

The ship's cargo was just some wooden boxes filled with earth. There was a delivery note attached to each of the boxes: *Property of Count Dracula, Carfax Abbey, Purfleet, near London.*

That night, Mina awoke with a cold draught blowing across her face. She sat up in bed and looked across to Lucy's bed. By the moonlight she could see the covers were thrown back. The bed was empty and the bedroom door was wide open.

Lucy must be sleep-walking again, thought Mina. It had been a habit of Lucy's for years. Mina hurried out of the bedroom to the hall. The front door was also wide open. She threw a shawl over her nightdress, grabbed another shawl for Lucy, and hurried out into the night.

Mina could see a dark figure in the distance, near the old abbey ruins. She hurried up the path. As she reached the old graveyard beside the abbey she saw Lucy lying on an old tomb. Standing over Lucy was a tall figure dressed in a black cloak. Its face was deadly white and its eyes burned red, like hot coals. As Mina ran towards them in terror, the tall, cloaked figure vanished into the night.

Lucy was still asleep. Mina woke her gently and put the shawl round her shoulders and fastened it at her throat with a large pin. Then the two friends made their way back to the house.

The next morning, Lucy looked pale. "I'm fine," she said when Mina asked how she felt, but there were two small red wounds on Lucy's neck.

"Oh, I'm sorry," said Mina. "I must have pricked you when I pinned your shawl last night."

The following night, Mina locked the bedroom door and shut the windows so that Lucy couldn't wander out of the house in her sleep. But that night Mina was woken by Lucy standing at the open window as if she was trying to get out, or let someone in. She was fast asleep.

During the day Lucy said she felt well, but she was very pale and seemed tired all the time. Mina couldn't help noticing that the two wounds on Lucy's neck hadn't healed.

That night, Mina woke to see a huge bat fluttering against the window. Lucy was opening the window, as if she was trying to let the creature in. Mina closed the window, firmly, and led Lucy gently back to bed.

The next morning, Mina received a disturbing letter from a convent in Budapest. I had been staying there for the last six weeks while I recovered from a dangerous fever. Mina decided that she must go to my side. She got a ticket for the next available train, and left Whitby later the same day.

Lucy's mother became so worried about her daughter's health that she wrote to Arthur, Lucy's fiancé. He arrived in Whitby within the week. He was shocked to see how ill Lucy was. She was thin, her skin was pale, and she was half-asleep by day and sleep-walking every night.

Lucy's mother and Arthur decided that it would be best to take Lucy home to London where she could be treated by Dr Jack Seward. He was an old friend of the family who had treated Lucy since she was young.

After examining Lucy, Dr Seward shook his head and put down his stethoscope. The two men left Lucy alone to rest.

The doctor spoke frankly to Arthur:

"I don't understand what's happening to Lucy. I think she has a blood disease, but I don't know how to treat it. But I do know someone who might be able to help."

"We'll try anything," said Arthur. "We just want Lucy to be well again."

Dr Seward patted him on the shoulder. He went out to send an urgent telegram to his old teacher, Professor Van Helsing:

COME AT ONCE.
A MATTER OF LIFE AND DEATH.

DR J SEWARD

Chapter Three
Lucy's Death

As soon as he saw Lucy, Professor Van Helsing pulled two lengths of rubber tubing and a small pump from his medical bag.

"Quickly," he said. "We haven't a moment to lose. Lucy must have a blood transfusion. Arthur, will you give Lucy some of your blood?"

"Of course," said Arthur. He rolled up his sleeve.

After the transfusion, Lucy looked better. A little colour had returned to her cheeks. She ate a little supper and went to bed early. But the next day she was deathly pale and tired again.

"Professor, could these have something to do with Lucy's illness?" asked Dr Seward. He pointed to the two small wounds that still gleamed on Lucy's neck.

"Why didn't you show me these marks before?" snapped the professor. "Lucy is in deadly danger. Arthur, go to the kitchen and bring me as much garlic as you can carry!"

Arthur shook his head in disbelief, but obeyed.

To our disbelief, Van Helsing hung a bunch of garlic bulbs at the window of Lucy's bedroom. He plaited the remaining garlic into a necklace which we hung around Lucy's neck. Then he went to see Lucy's mother.

"You must sleep in Lucy's room tonight," the professor told her. "Lock the door and don't let anyone in until morning. Lucy's life may depend upon it."

That night, Lucy's mother went to Lucy's bedroom. She locked the door behind her, just as Van Helsing had told her.

"Oooh, dear! What's that awful smell?" she said to herself. "Garlic? What's that nasty stuff doing here? Lucy needs fresh air!"

She pulled the garlic bulbs from the handles and opened the window.

Instantly there came a howl from outside, like the cry of a dog or wolf. There was a rush of icy wind that woke Lucy. She sat up in bed just as an enormous wolf leapt through the window.

Lucy's mother screamed. Her chest felt like a red iron band was crushing it. She gasped and fell to the ground, but as she was falling she clutched the garlic necklace around Lucy's neck. The necklace broke and the garlic fell to the ground. Lucy screamed as the enormous wolf, with a triumphant howl, leapt onto her bed.

CHAPTER FOUR
LUCY RETURNS

But let me return briefly to my own story. It is linked to Lucy's, as you will see.

I eventually managed to break the lock on Count Dracula's gates and escaped. The local priest found me wandering in the forest, half-crazed with fever and muttering about terrible things. He took me to the convent in Budapest where the nuns nursed me back to health.

Your mother, Mina, arrived soon after my recovery, and we decided to waste no more time. We were married in the convent with the nuns as our witnesses. Soon we returned to London to begin our married life.

The day after the wolf attack, Professor Van Helsing came to our London home.

"I have bad news," he said. "Very bad news. Lucy and her mother are dead."

Mina gasped. Tears sprang into her eyes.

"But I need your help, both of you," Van Helsing continued. "You were good friends to Lucy when she was alive. Will you still help her now she's dead?"

"Of course we were good friends. I was her best friend," said Mina. "But what do you mean: help her now she's dead?"

"Lucy may be dead," said Van Helsing, "but she is not at rest. Please help me give her peace."

That night, I went with Professor Van Helsing to the churchyard where Lucy had been buried in her family tomb. Mina stayed at home. Arthur and Dr Seward met us at the gate and we made our way through the maze of graves until we reached the tomb. We lifted the heavy stone lid. Lucy's mother's coffin lay in the tomb. But the lid of Lucy's coffin was flung back. The coffin was empty.

"Where is she?" asked Arthur, his voice trembling.

"Here I am," said a voice behind us. "And I am hungry for your blood, my darling!"

The creature looked like Lucy, but when it smiled its teeth were long and pointed.

"No!" shouted Arthur. "Whatever you are, be gone!"

The creature laughed and seemed to melt back into the tomb. We looked down. The thing that lay in Lucy's coffin looked like Lucy, but it was smiling and its smile showed its sharp teeth. On its lips was fresh blood.

Professor Van Helsing opened his medical bag and took out a sharpened stake made of ash wood. He handed the stake to Arthur.

"You loved her better than anyone else, so you must do it," said Van Helsing.

"Do what?" asked Arthur.

"Drive this stake into her heart," said the professor. "It's the only way to stop this monster – this vampire – that has taken over Lucy's body." He pushed the stake into Arthur's hands. "This is the only way to get rid of the monster and let the real Lucy rest in peace."

After a moment's hesitation, Arthur lifted

the stake high above his head, then plunged it down into Lucy's chest. There was a scream and then silence.

We watched as Lucy's face changed. The sharp fangs vanished and so did the blood stain on her lips. The final look of pain disappeared. It was Lucy's face once more, not a monster's.

"Now she is at peace," said Van Helsing.

Chapter Five
Mina in Deadly Danger

We trudged back across the moonlit graveyard.

"At last it is all over," Arthur said, breaking the silence.

"No!" said Van Helsing. "We have cured only one victim. We must destroy the source of the vampire disease, Count Dracula himself. He cannot bear daylight. When morning comes he must return to the earth of his own grave to sleep. We must find his hiding place."

I started at the familiar name. "But I know where he is!" I said. "I went to Romania to help Dracula buy an old house in Purfleet, near London. It's known as Carfax Abbey, because the ruins of the old abbey surround the house."

"We don't have a minute to lose!" cried Van Helsing. He seized his medical bag.

"We must find the monster's resting place and put an end to him!"

A bitter wind was blowing around the old house as we arrived. The house stood in the grounds of a ruined abbey. Around the abbey was a graveyard, and in the middle of the graveyard was an old chapel. Arthur and Dr Seward lit burning torches. Van Helsing and I followed them through the ancient graveyard to the chapel.

In the darkened chapel were the boxes of earth I'd seen in the courtyard of Castle Dracula.

"Pull off the lids!" Van Helsing ordered.

Arthur, Dr Seward and I levered off the heavy wooden lids. Van Helsing reached into his bag and brought out handfuls of holy wafers. "We must scatter these in each of the boxes."

We did as he said. As soon as the wafers touched the ancient earth, a foul smell of damp and decay rose into the air.

"Has that destroyed the fiend?" asked Arthur.

Van Helsing looked around. "Give me a torch," he said. He held the torch over the floor. There was a mark on the floor where a box had been resting, but it was no longer there.

"He's tricked us again!" said Van Helsing. "He's hidden the last box. We must find it before he can infect anyone else, just as he did poor Lucy."

We searched the ruins and the house, but there was no sign of the missing box.

~

The four of us returned to the house Mina and I shared just as the first light of dawn was reddening the sky. As I stepped out of Arthur's carriage, I looked up at our bedroom window. I could see the shadow of a tall cloaked figure against the window.

"Look!" I cried.

The figure turned. Even from the street I could see its eyes burning like red coals.

"It's him. It's Dracula!"

The four of us rushed up the stairs. I threw open the bedroom door. Mina was kneeling on the floor. Standing above her was Count Dracula. His lips and chin were smeared with blood.

Van Helsing pulled a wooden crucifix
from his bag. Holding the crucifix in front
of him, he strode towards Dracula.

"Be gone!" Van Helsing cried. "Go back to
Hell, where you belong!"

Dracula snarled, "I will have my revenge!"
He leapt through the window. I ran after
him, but all I could see was a bat, fluttering
away in the distance.

I turned back to Mina. She had two red marks on her neck.

Van Helsing stepped forward. In his hand was a holy wafer.

"*In nomine Patris...et Filii...et Spiritus Sancti,*" he murmured. He pressed the wafer against Mina's forehead. She screamed and fell. On her forehead, where the wafer had been pressed, was a crimson burn mark.

Van Helsing crouched beside her. "Mina, can you hear me?" he asked.

"Yes," replied Mina.

"Where is Dracula?" asked Van Helsing.

Mina groaned. She tossed her head violently from side to side.

"A boat...Varna."

"Varna is a port," said Van Helsing. "It's on the coast of the Black Sea. Dracula is trying to return home to his castle. We must catch him before he does."

Mina opened her eyes. "Help me," she begged. "Stop me becoming a vampire."

Chapter Six
Peace at Last

Van Helsing, Arthur, Dr Seward, Mina and I
caught the next boat to France. Then we
travelled across Europe by train. It was our
only chance to catch Dracula, as his boat
would take longer than our train. We would
reach Romania before him, or so we hoped.

Throughout the long journey, Mina slept
all day but was awake all night. While the
others slept, she stared out of the train
window into the darkness as if watching or
listening for something. The crimson burn
on her forehead still glowed and the wounds
on her neck had not healed. I feared that
even if we caught Dracula and destroyed
him, it was too late for Mina. She had
become what she most feared: a vampire.

It was early November when we crossed
the border from Hungary into Romania.
The snow was lying thickly on the ground.

At the border we hired horses, thick tents and furs, then we took the road to Bistritz. As we rode, we looked for any signs of a heavy wagon having driven along the road before us. There were none.

We reached Castle Dracula in three days. The snow lay in drifts blocking the road. We dismounted and led our horses through the thick snow and up the steep winding path to the castle.

There were no wheel marks, and no footprints. The castle gates were open, just as I'd left them so many months before. There was no sign of anyone.

We set up camp in the forest. We built a
fire for Mina and Van Helsing spread a
circle of holy wafers around her tent. Then
he took out three ash stakes.

"We must find the three vampires who
nearly captured you," he said to me.

I led the way into the castle cellars.

In the darkness were the three female
vampires, asleep in three ancient coffins.
One by one we drove a stake into each body.
As we did, their bodies crumbled into dust.

When we returned to our camp, night was falling. Mina was shivering, but not with cold. By the light of the blazing fire I could see her eyes were wide with fear.

"He is near now, I can sense it," she said.

Suddenly, we heard the rumble of a cart.

We mounted our horses just as the cart came around a bend in the road. We forced our terrified horses into the road. When the driver saw us he tried to swerve. The cart skidded in the snow and overturned. A wooden box fell from the back of the cart, hit the road and fell open. There lay Dracula as if asleep.

Just as the Sun vanished, Van Helsing drew out a stake. Dracula's eyes opened. Van Helsing held the stake over Dracula's chest, then plunged it in deep.

Dracula screamed. But like the three female vampires, as soon as the stake entered his heart, Dracula's body started to crumble away. In seconds, Dracula was dust.

"Is he dead?"

We turned to see Mina walking towards us. Arthur lit a torch and held it over the box. Van Helsing reached into his bag and began scattering holy wafers onto the soil.

"He will never drink innocent blood again," said Van Helsing.

By the light of the torch I could see that the burn-shaped scar on Mina's forehead and the bite marks on her neck had vanished. She was safe; safe from the evil spell of Dracula. She was not a vampire.

POST SCRIPT

And that, my dearest Lucy, is the story of how you got your name. And perhaps, now you know the truth, you won't tease me when I check every night that all the windows of our house are locked and barred even during the hottest of summers. And perhaps you will understand why I insist that you and your brothers have a crucifix above your beds. For though it is twenty years since we destroyed Dracula, I still dream of wolves howling and of huge bats whose leathery wings clatter and batter at our windows.

Bram Stoker (1847–1912)

Abraham (Bram) Stoker was born in Dublin on 8 November 1847. He was ill as a child which left him unable to walk, and he spent much of his childhood in bed. He later acknowledged that this time helped to

Bram Stoker

develop his creativity and imagination.

Stoker left school with honours in maths. He started working as a civil servant but was more interested in the theatre, and started writing play reviews for the *Dublin Evening Mail*. His work was widely respected, and it brought him to the attention of the famous actor, Henry Irving. The two men became friends, and in 1878 Stoker moved to London to manage Irving's Lyceum Theatre.

Stoker juggled his stage work with writing. His first published novel, *The Snake's Pass*, appeared in 1890 and had elements of horror and the supernatural, which were developed in his next and most famous work, *Dracula*. Stoker continued to write until his death on 20 April 1912.

DRACULA (1897)

Before writing *Dracula*, Stoker spent a long time researching European vampire folklore. He originally called the novel *The Un-Dead* and changed the title only a few weeks before publication to *Dracula*, which means 'dragon' or 'devil' in Romanian. Count Dracula's appearance and mannerisms were broadly based on those of Henry Irving.

Dracula was well received on publication. However, it was only in the 20th century that the film versions made it become as popular and well-known as it is today.

Titles in the CLASSICS RETOLD series:

978 1 4451 0461 4 pb
978 1 4451 0818 6 eBook

978 1 4451 0460 7 pb
978 1 4451 0815 5 eBook

978 1 4451 0458 4 pb
978 1 4451 0819 3 eBook

978 1 4451 0462 1 pb
978 1 4451 0817 9 eBook

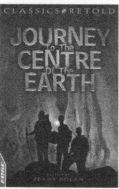

978 1 4451 0459 1 pb
978 1 4451 0816 2 eBook

978 1 4451 0457 7 pb
978 1 4451 0820 9 eBook